HUE BOY

For Leann and Brian
R.P.M.

For Enid and for Wilf
C.B.

PUFFIN PIED PIPER BOOKS
Published by the Penguin Group
Penguin Books USA Inc., 375 Hudson Street, New York, New York, 10014, U.S.A.
Penguin Books Ltd, 27 Wrights Lane, London W8 5TZ, England
Penguin Books Australia Ltd, Ringwood, Victoria, Australia
Penguin Books Canada Ltd, 10 Alcorn Avenue, Toronto, Ontario, Canada M4V 3B2
Penguin Books (N. Z.) Ltd, 182–190 Wairau Road, Auckland 10, New Zealand
Penguin Books Ltd, Registered Offices: Harmondsworth, Middlesex, England

First published in hardcover in the United States 1993 by
Dial Books for Young Readers
A Division of Penguin Books USA Inc.
Published in Great Britain by Victor Gollancz Ltd
Text copyright © 1993 by Rita Phillips Mitchell
Pictures copyright © 1993 by Caroline Binch
All rights reserved
Library of Congress Catalog Number: 92-18560
Printed in Hong Kong
First Puffin Pied Piper Printing 1997
ISBN 0-14-055995-7
1 3 5 7 9 10 8 6 4 2

A Pied Piper Book is a registered trademark of
Dial Books for Young Readers, a division of Penguin Books USA Inc.,
® TM 1,163,686 and ® TM 1,054,312.

HUE BOY
is also available in hardcover from
Dial Books for Young Readers.

HUE BOY

Rita Phillips Mitchell

pictures by
Caroline Binch

A Puffin Pied Piper

Little Hue Boy was big news in his village. He was so small that all his friends towered over him. Every morning Hue Boy's mama measured him.

"Come, I must measure you before you go to school," she said. "Stand straight against the wall."

It did not matter how straight Hue Boy stood, he remained the same size—very small. He didn't grow at all, at all.

"Oh lawd!" cried Hue Boy's mama. "I wish your papa was home. He would know what to do about this."

But Hue Boy knew his papa was working on a ship, far away.

Then one day Mama said, "Hue Boy, if you want to grow tall, you must eat fresh vegetables and fruit every day."

"Like pumpkins?" said Hue Boy. "I like pumpkin soup."

"Pumpkins are good. But what about spinach, Hue Boy?"

"Yuck!" Hue Boy said. "I don't like spinach, Mama!
I'd rather have fruit, like mangoes and melons."

"And pineapples and sapodillas, I suppose?"
said his mama.

"Mm, yum, yum," said Hue Boy.

"How about sweetsops, cashews, and craboos?"
his mama asked.

"Yes!" said Hue Boy. "And don't forget guavas
or tamarinds, either."

"I won't, Hue Boy," said Mama.

Hue Boy was soon eating
everything his mama gave him.
Pumpkin soup was delicious,
but he enjoyed eating
fruit best.

Still, Hue Boy didn't
grow one little bit.
He didn't grow at all,
at all.

On Hue Boy's birthday Gran gave him a special present.
"I've made you new clothes," she said. "You'll soon grow into them."

Hue Boy tried on the clothes. They felt a little loose.
"Lawdy! You look taller already," said Gran.

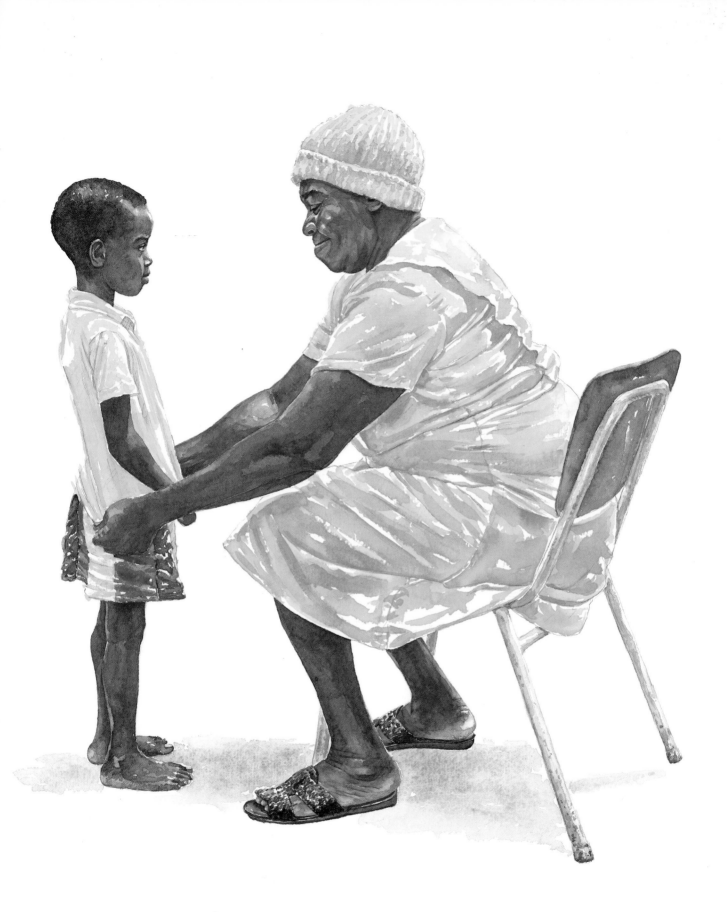

Then one morning their
neighbor Carlos said, "I know,
Hue Boy. Some stretching
exercises will do the trick.
Ten minutes a day. That's all
you need to do."

And so Hue Boy began to do
all sorts of exercises. He stretched
as much as he could.

Still, Hue Boy didn't grow one
little bit. He didn't grow at all,
at all.

At school his classmates chanted:
  "Heels, heels, high-heeled shoes,
    Needed for the smallest boy in school."
Hue Boy looked down. But Miss Harper the teacher said,

"Stuff and nonsense! Just ignore them, Hue Boy. You'll be growing soon enough."

Still, Hue Boy didn't grow one little bit. He didn't grow at all, at all.

Mama was worried. "I don't like you being teased, Hue Boy," she said. "Come, we must look for some help."

First they went to see the wisest man in the village. "Please," said Mama, "can you help Hue Boy to grow like other children?"

The wise man looked at Hue Boy from head to toe. Then from toe to head. "Well, Hue Boy," he said. "Where help is not needed, no help can be given."

Next they visited Doctor Gamas. He examined Hue Boy thoroughly. Then he said, "There is absolutely nothing wrong with you, Hue Boy. Some people are short and perfectly healthy, you know."

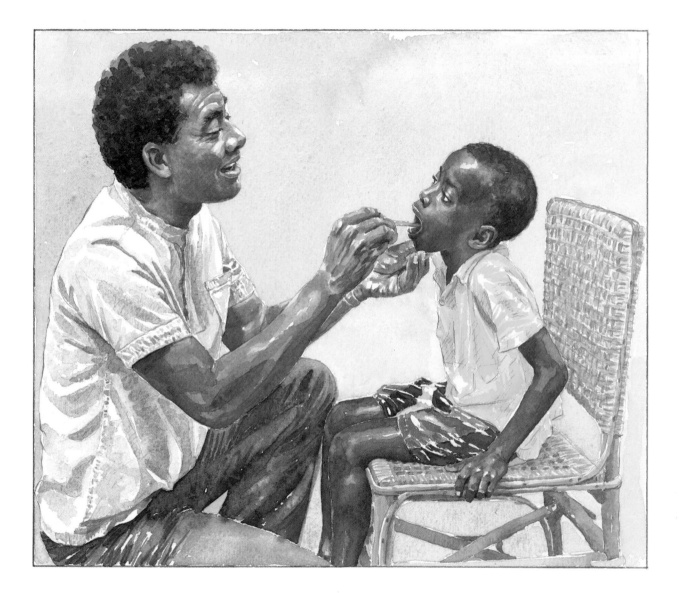

"Lawdy," cried Mama. "This problem seems to be bigger than this village!" She thought carefully. "We ought to try Miss Frangipani the healer," she said. "Maybe she can help."

Hue Boy sighed. "I hope so."

"Miss Frangipani," said Mama.
"Please! Can you do something for
Hue Boy to make him grow?"
    "No problem," said Miss Frangipani.
"I alone hold the secret to growing!"
    Miss Frangipani placed a hand on
Hue Boy's head and said:

"Ooooo! Ooooo!
Grow-o, Grow-o.
A touch of the hand,
A wish of the mind,
Comes the cure from far away.
Ooooo! Ooooo!
Grow-o, Grow-o.
As you're meant to do."

    Then Miss Frangipani gave
Hue Boy a bundle of herbs.
    "You must have your bath
with these," she told him.
"Mind you do it every night."

For a month Hue Boy did everything that he had been told. Still, Hue Boy didn't grow one little bit. He didn't grow at all, at all.

Sometimes Hue Boy liked to go
to the harbor. Here he watched the
ships come and go, and he could
forget about his size.
  One day a beautiful big ship came in.
  Man, that looks good! thought Hue Boy.
It's the biggest ship I ever saw!

Then he saw a very tall man among the passengers. The tall man walked straight toward him.
"Hello, Hue Boy," he said.
"Papa!" cried Hue Boy.

His father took Hue Boy's hand and they walked away from the harbor and into the village.

They walked past Miss Frangipani.
They walked past Doctor Gamas and the wisest
man in the village.
They walked past Miss Harper and Carlos.
And they walked past Hue Boy's friends from school.
Then they met Gran and Mama.

And Hue Boy walked tall, with his head held high.
He was the happiest boy in the village.

And he didn't feel small at all, at all.

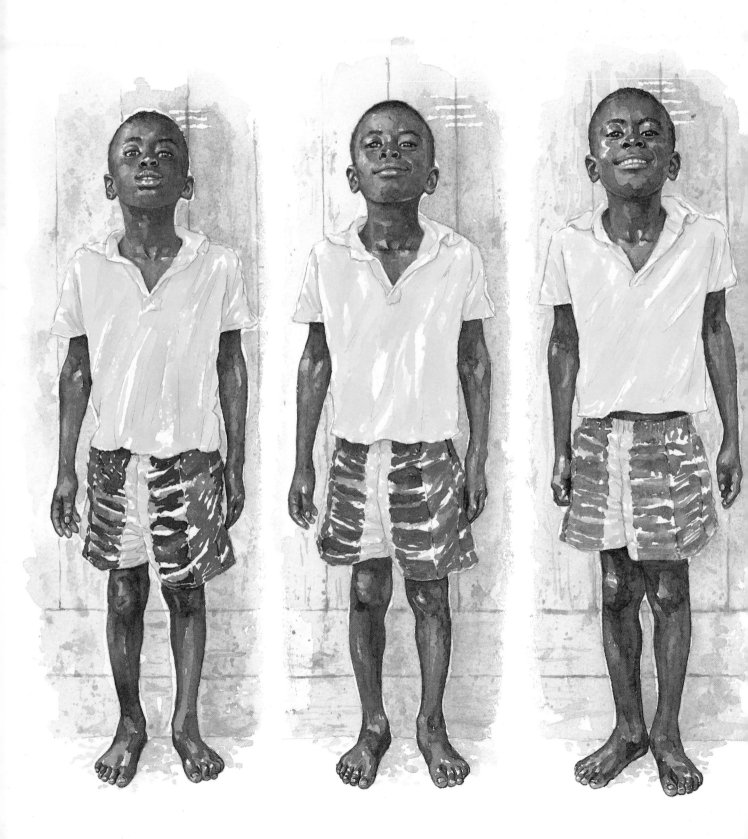

Rita Phillips Mitchell was born and reared in Belize, which borders on the Caribbean, and has worked as a teacher, principal, and counselor for many years. *Hue Boy* was inspired by the experience of a young nephew in Belize. Ms. Mitchell lives in London with her husband, and has one grown-up son.

Caroline Binch illustrated the much-acclaimed *Amazing Grace* (Dial) by Mary Hoffman. Among its many honors, *Amazing Grace* was an *American Bookseller* Pick of the Lists, a *Booklist* Editors' Choice, one of *School Library Journal*'s Best Books, an ALA Notable Children's Book, and a *Reading Rainbow* Feature Selection. Ms. Binch is a painter and photographer who has traveled widely, especially in the Caribbean. She and her young son live in Cornwall, England.